Hummingbird

and the Little People
(and a VERY big person too)

Written by Elizabeth Albert-Peacock
Illustrations by Anna Granholm

The story begins.

Hummingbird (Nenookass) loved the outdoors and walking in the woods. One time she had all day to do whatever she wanted. She asked her mother (ni maa maa), "What do you need help with today?"

Mother said, "You have been such a good little girl my Hummingbird. Today is your day to do whatever you want."

There was
so much to
see and do.

Hummingbird knew there
were new pollywogs in
the creek that ran behind
their house and that the
caterpillars were
beginning
to turn
into
butterflies (memengwaag).

Dragonflies flew about. The lightning bugs were just starting to blink in the early evening and the flowers were opening up on warm days. Early summer is for babies to be born in the forest too. Maybe she'd come upon one or two. Today would be one of those days!

"Mother, I'm off to play in the forest. I'll see you later! Bye!"

Mother gave her a hug and told her to be careful. Her little brother (nishime) Josh wanted to come along but she said, "Not this time Josh. Next time, I promise."

So on that early summer day, she followed a squirrel (ajidamoo), jumping from branch to branch, hoping she would find where the squirrel had built a nest so she just might see baby squirrels. She had never seen a baby squirrel. She knew that robins (opichi) laid their eggs as she had seen them building their nests. Maybe she would even see a fawn (gidagaakoons), or catch a glimpse of a raccoon (esiban). Once, she had seen a porcupine (gaag) climbing a tree, ever so slowly.

She went further and further in the woods trying to keep up, but soon the squirrel disappeared and she couldn't find it.

"Hey squirrel, where did you go?" She said.

It wasn't long before she realized she was lost. She called out, but no one answered.

"Ni maa maa! Indede! (Mother! Father!)"

She tried to find the path, but to no avail. She wished she had marked it somehow.

Soon enough she came to an opening in the woods.

And then she heard something. Tiny voices. Tiny laughter.

Then she saw them. The little people (memegwesiwag). They were so small she probably could have held one in her hand! She had heard stories about them but had never seen them. They were talking and laughing and spoke the same language as her people.

An early morning rain
had created puddles
and the little people
were jumping in them.
One was sailing on a leaf,
another sliding down
the ant (enigoons) hills
on acorn tops. Several
were swinging on
flowers and dropping
into the puddles. Others
watched, sitting on
dandelion tops.

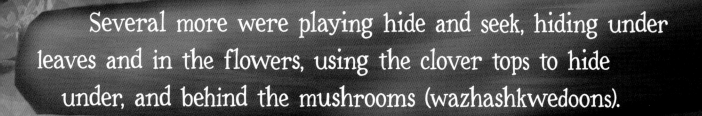

Several more were playing hide and seek, hiding under leaves and in the flowers, using the clover tops to hide under, and behind the mushrooms (wazhashkwedoons).

They were having so much fun!

They were laughing with the chipmunks (agongos) and singing with the birds (bineshiinhwag). There were too many to count!

She saw a little girl riding on a hummingbird,

and another on a bee (aamoo)! The humming sounds were amazing.

Some of the little people were dancing
(niimi'idiwag). They formed a large circle and did
a round dance (niimi'idi).

Hummingbird remembered the round dance from
a powwow that she had gone to last summer. Her
family spent the summer camping and traveling
the powwow trail.

Mother was a jingle dress dancer and had made dresses for Hummingbird and herself. Father had made her beaded moccasins. Grandmother (Nookomis) had made her a shawl and hair ties with feathers. Grandfather (Mishoomis) had given her a small tobacco (asemaa) pouch that he had made for her. Her little brother Josh used his allowance to buy her a barrette for her hair. She had a beautiful outfit for the powwows.

Listening to the beautiful humming, she began to sing and dance to the amazing music! Suddenly, the little people heard and saw her and they began to run and hide. She called to them, "Please come back. I won't hurt you."

One of the little people responded, "We are afraid of humans. That is why we run and hide."

"Please," Hummingbird said to them, "don't be afraid of me. I am not here to cause any harm. I'm lost, you see. I can't find my way home. It is I who am afraid."

The little people became very quiet and listened to her. And they slowly started peeking from behind the mushrooms and came closer to look at her.

They saw her big smile and realized that she was not going to hurt them. Hummingbird sat down and one of them asked her, "Are you hungry?"

"Yes, I sure am" she said, and they brought her things to eat. Strawberries, and hazelnuts. They offered mushrooms but she grimaced. Her mother always told her to never eat the mushrooms in the forest.

"You need to know what mushrooms one can eat and those that can make you very ill. You have a lot to learn about mushrooms, so don't eat them please!" They brought her some nectar they had made from the flowers. It was so good and sweet.

"Do you like it?" one of them asked.

"Yes," she said, "It is delicious!"

Soon enough she was no longer thirsty or hungry.

"Do you think," she asked, "you could help me find my way home?"

"Please?" She asked again.

It had been a long day. She became very tired and sat under a big cedar tree to rest and soon she fell fast asleep.

While she was asleep the little people came up with a plan to help their new friend. They sent their runners even deeper into the forest to find someone who could quickly take Hummingbird home.

When she finally awakened, a very large hairy man was carrying her. She recognized him from pictures.

It was Sabe (saw-bay). He is known by other names. Bigfoot. Sasquatch. Abominable Snowman. Yeti.

She had heard the elders talk about a giant hairy man that looked a bit like an ape or hairy human and that he was a messenger of warning, telling the people they needed to change their ways.

She was very afraid, of course, even though he was surprisingly gentle.

"Sabe, she said, "you aren't going to hurt me, are you?"

He answered a bit gruffly, but his eyes were gentle. "No little one. I'm carrying you home to your family."

She let out a big sigh.

The little people were traveling along with them, riding on the backs of mice (waawaabiganoojiinhyag) and chipmunks. The smallest of them rode on hummingbirds and bees.

Soon enough, Sabe stopped at the edge of the forest. Hummingbird could see her house in the distance. Then Sabe gently put her down. She stepped out into the open and then turned toward her new friends.

"Thank you (Miigwech)," she said to Sabe. She gave him a hug around his leg. He gave her the biggest smile she had ever seen.

"And, thank you," she said to all the little people, who all had gathered around Sabe. She smiled and reached down, gently offering her hand in friendship.

Then she turned and ran home.

She couldn't wait to tell her family about her adventure! What a day to remember, a day with the little people and Sabe, dancing and sharing food, having a visit on a beautiful early summer day.

Mother, Father, Grandmother, Grandfather and her little brother Josh, were waiting for her. They and the whole village had been looking for her and were overjoyed to see her.

Josh saw her first. "Hummingbird! Hummingbird!"

Grandmother ran to hug her, saying, "My girl, my girl! Oh Hummingbird, we have been so worried. You were gone for so long. What were you doing? You must be hungry and tired."

At that she laughed and told them, "You are never going to believe where I've been and what happened to me! Please sit and listen to my adventure!"

And so, the story began.

Glossary

Ant • enigoons

Bee • aamoo

Bigfoot • Sabe (pronounced 'saw•bay')

Birds • bineshiinhwag

Butterfly • memengwaa
(memengwaag) plural

Chipmunk • agongos

Dance • niimi

Dancing • niimi'idiwag

Father • indede

Fawn • gidagaakoons

Grandmother • nookomis

Grandfather •mishoomis

Hazelnuts • bagaan

Hummingbird • Nenookaas (name),
or nenookaasi

Little Brother • nishime

Little People • memegwesiwag

Mice • waawaabiganoojiinhyag

Mother • ni maa maa

Mushroom • wazhashkwedoons

Porcupine • gaag

Raccoon • esiban

Robin • opichi

Squirrel • ajidamoo

Strawberries • ode'imin

Thank you • miigwech

Tobacco • asemaa

To our beautiful grandchildren, when you think over the events of each day, ask yourself, did I make a difference? May you always be proud of who you are, and grateful for all your blessings. Love you always and forever, Nana

Hummingbird and the Little People (and a VERY big person too)
© 2022 Written by Elizabeth Albert-Peacock, Illustrations by Anna Granholm

ISBN 979-8-9851527-8-4

Book cover and interior design by Paul Nylander | Illustrada

Black Bears and Blueberries Publishing
www.blackbearsandblueberries.com

A Native owned non-profit publishing company, with a focus on creating and developing Native children's books for all young people written by Native authors and illustrators.